MIND WHAT YOU TELL YOUR DAUGHTER

AINCRE
MAAME-FOSUA
EVANS

Illustrated by Kuukua Wilson
Edited by Sailesh Naidu

To my Mother,
to whom I owe my best parts.
Thank you for planting seeds
that have only just begun to blossom.

CONTENTS

FOR THE READER

ɔbaa na ɔwo ɔbarima.

It is a woman that gives birth to a man

- Akan Proverb

FOR THE READER

Poetry allows the reader a creative entry point into the complex representations of ordinary people. These realities are not just complex but disruptive; they challenge the reader to theorize through connection that is often involuntary and bodily. Poetry and fiction in this way are central to our radical imagination.

Writing this first collection of poetry has been a deeply disruptive, mindful and restorative process. It has taken me years to gently tease out what I have been trying to pull. I do not mean to tell a collective story or assume vague notions of sisterhood in the pages that follow. There is no collective story I could write alone, nor would I try to. 'Mind what you tell your daughter' is a collection that puts on trial the difficult and contentious claim, that what we teach and tell our daughters is for their own protection. We not only accommodate violence through these lessons but we soak our children and burn them in it. I hope the collection speaks with you at whatever moment these words find you.

PART I: Learning silence

NOT AN EXPERIENCE

You touch my skin and it pricks.
These are not hands that hold my worth.
You drink me in,

but there is sin in your guzzle,

rot on your tongue.

I refuse to be,
deserving of your touch

but not your affection.

WHOLE

In the Adinkra,

the Northern Star is female.

My cousin tells me that she sits above the moon

and her shine is what drove the Sun to envy.

That her light was so beautiful, God could not bear to

look at her

and so he placed her far away in the night.

I have often thought of plucking her from her darkness

and eating her whole.

SPINACH AND CASSAVA

Imaa and I have walked twice around this garden
passed the plantain leaves and pawpaw fruit;
spinach leaves and cassava she had once knelt down to
plant
coconut trees she had tended to,
beaten me sore for climbing.
I cannot bring myself to speak to her,
she cannot reply.
But she clasps her fingers in my own
and grips me through the dementia.
Shakily we walk around,
and each time we pass the coconuts,
she smiles.

SCENTS FROM THE SOUTH ATLANTIC

On Tuesdays, the fishermen do not fish.
Their nets cast down shadows on the sand.
On Tuesday's the ocean is naked,
they say that she has cursed the day itself
and banished those who trespass her sands.
So they honour her peace.

On Tuesdays, the fishermen do not fish.
They return to their wives
who taste of salt and smoked tilapia.
They smell of an ocean
with no trespasses.

ACCOMMODATE

You teach your daughter to say yes.
So often, that by sixteen it slips off her tongue
like a bad habit.
So often, that when it's time for her to say no,
even when her very life depends on it,
she can't.

MAGICIANS

Adwoa has come to tell us -
tell us of something strange.
She is excited in her lack of understanding,
her smile is wide but her hands uneasy.
She says she sat on Uncle Kweku's lap
when Auntie Esi had left the room.
He had told her to rock gently-
slowly from side to side,
so that a cane in his trousers
jumped out from thin air

and pushed against her thigh.
So sure was she of his magic
that her smile beamed through chipped teeth.
But we had seen Adwoa's hands
yes her hands were like our hands -
telling,
sweating off our limbs,
the first time we sat

on a magician's lap.

TO DAUGHTERS WHO WERE ASKED FOR MORE

When young girls go about greeting
they subdue themselves to a whisper.

We speak when spoken to amongst elders,
and retrieve what we are asked to bring.

It is understood that in the company of men
we set but do not sit at the table.

We are there to retrieve
and we pray that what they ask for
is water.

TRADITION

And so is it just daughters, for whom culture's noose
tightens its knot

DAISIES

This world plucks little black girls apart
like a child tears daisies from their limbs
with my sisters we heard them
we were sat right there
five white boys
laughing in the way they do.
Laughing in the way we cannot.

Each making a pact
to *fuck* a black girl by semester's end
to pry one open and to see what is inside
the words washed up on my mind as glass does in sand
and for weeks my thoughts were stranded.
I suppose I should have seen it coming
when years later she came to me
whispered what she had done
what she had *tried to do*
I tell her that this world threw her away
long before she tried to leave it
she told me that the world had forced itself between her
legs
and pried her open.

SOFT REJECTIONS

You are strong-
my mother tells me

Her lips pressed to my temple
her knuckles are bruised,
knotted in scars.
I hear the sides of her ankles
Swell beneath us

You are strong –
my friends tell me

Rehearsing the words
poured over them
with tongues still unconvinced.

You are strong
I repeat to myself

But the words are far
too heavy for my starving soul.
It spits them back out at me,
with bile.

FOR ACTIONS THAT ARE INEXCUSABLE

Eyes on the floor
she came to us.
She said she knew he was wrong but that
he loved her.
His mother's mouth had told her
that he did.

We told her there were many men
Who loved her
Whose eyes will get to love her
Men who should count themselves lucky
To hear her God
wash their name
off her tongue

We told her that being loved is not the ceiling
Whispered that it is far from our skies.

So what if he loves you?
Tell him that his love sits boring
On a mouth that has forgotten
The taste of his name

PART II – Rain in the Harmattan

BEHIND WOODEN RAILINGS

My brother's eyes do not leave me.
They teethe with injustice and scorn.
Anger that comes from immobility
stolen agency.

I sit upstairs.
Hands curled around wooden railings that I trust will
protect my senses from the scene.
But his gaze streams through as sunlight might at
Harmattan back home,

as sunlight might
back home.

Beside him two policemen,
tall,
white,
armed,
apologetic.
They tell my mother there was a mistake,
they had been looking for a black man
but had mistaken this black boy

for someone else.
For some other mother's black boy.

He turned away from me then.
his eyes ripped from mine.

and in the rupture

my world curled into a scream.
I had seen something too intimate -
far too sharp for our bond,

far too heavy for still soft hands.

In his face there was humiliation and pain.
More than I had never thought to see.

More than I was supposed to.

In the moment his eyes turned from me
something between us shifted.

Much like my hands did on those railings.
I have never forgiven myself
for curling up behind them,
and I believe neither of us
have loved our eyes

quite the same since.

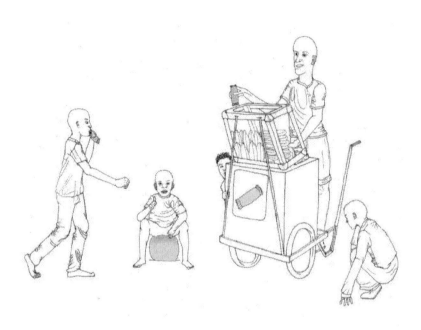

FOR BOYS AND THEIR SOFTNESS

Your son is not rough around the edges.
Seedlings are not born with bark.

HEAT

Last night I think I spoke to God.
Her voice reached out to me
and she waded out to my soul.
I touched her presence
as my fingers ventured further.
If calmness could have a heat
such a touch would be her own.
In her gaze she called me to her
but I could not go.
I asked her if she were God
she replied she is my God,
for she lives in me,
and has made my light her home.
With her hand she called me to her
but I could not go.
I asked her if she were woman
she replied she is my God
and in me a woman she remains.

THE LENGTH OF US

Ama cannot describe what she likes.
She has never explored the length of her body.
Not once has she danced by herself,

in herself.

Your cousin tells her that there are men
who love an untouched woman.
A woman who cannot say what she likes
and what she doesn't.

RECIPROCITY

I took her cheek to mine and told her,
that if I were a whisper
then in this world she were surely air.
That if my soul were made of moon
her being had kissed each of my faces
until they shone in turn.
Her coils in my hands, she kissed me
and in her touch she drummed it too.
She said,
if in this world
dust took human form
she would be powder
and I, sandstorm.

WESTERN GAZE

Violence is native to
Western eyes
and so I chose long ago
to never see myself
through them.

I chose long ago
to never inhale storms
whose winds

do not belong inside me.

ODE TO MY HIPS

My hips sway as I walk.
As sure as palm trees swing in the shade
my hips jump like palm wine shakes
and oh so many men
drunk on their taste,
have thanked God in-between them

SHEA BUTTER

Your niece's body has been touched by hands
she had never wanted to know.

Hands that eat from the same plate, in turn.
Her mother has stopped reminding her
to oil her skin after bathing.
She does not want the marks
to catch the light outside.

WHEN WORDS FOLLOW

There are women who search for conversations,
for words they hope to share.
They chase them into bed-sheets,
on mattresses laid bare.
They shadow behind locked
doors that are sure to stay closed,
and believe that after,
after they have been
spread out on their backs
like cloth on ironing board racks,
after the commotion
after the flight
they might,
in the silence that precedes
in the aftermath of it all,
finally find the conversation
that explains it.

WINTERS IN WEST AFRICA

You say you have lived through winters;
that you have cursed the cold
Have sacrificed weeks to the weather back home.
That there is nothing that seers like the prick of ice on
skin.

Skin.
I tell you I have heard my sister recount me stories,
written with pencil on paper

Lined paper.
Tales of what men have done to her *Skin*

Skin I have bathed,

Skin that I have prayed up against.
I may not know the prick of ice on my arms
But your coldest winters might not compare
to the winters I have slept through
deep in West Africa

WHAT MY UNCLE DID

She crawled towards my mother,
her hand tore at her winter coat.
At the door she begged for her sister -
reaching out with one hand.
wedding ring on wet fingers,
hand under pregnant belly
cradling my cousin from her pain.
My mother dropped to the concrete
to carry her younger sister
and together we went inside the house.
Their wailing plucked my hairs.
It burst my drums.
It stole my voice.
The way their tears streamed that day,
like rain falls on tin roofs.

I cursed God under my breath
and I knew I could not forgive him.

A TREE

My Uncle said,
good men must let a woman breathe.
if you see a beautiful flower
*"You must not pick it,
you must not pick it!"*
he would say.

But Uncle,
I am no beautiful flower.
I am a tree
rooted so deep
you could not pick me
if you tried.

COLLECTING DUST

My mind is not a thing to be adorned
from afar like hand-made cloth
that lays as a gift in your house
collecting dust
where it sits.

No my mind is not a thing
to brag about with company
that has never once asked my take

No my mind is not a thing
to be placed next to you
with my degrees lined up in order
to compliment your being
but never my own.
No my mind is not a thing
not a thing
not a thing at all.

WHAT MEN HAVE THOUGHT TO EMPTY

To the men with soft hands
who loved me with care,
with honey and compassion, and fortitude.
For the men who had,
with all the intention some women hope for,
emptied out a space in their lives
just for me.

To the men whose mothers hands I have greeted,
whose sister's cheeks I have kissed;
an apology.
I am sorry.
I did not know I could not bend into spaces that
did not hold me

I promise you I have broken my bones
and bled out my tears

trying to want
what some women hope for.
But I do not want to fit into spaces
that men have thought to empty
even if
just for me.

PART III – Touching discomfort

SEEDS FROM YOUR MOTHER

Your mother hands you lessons
with which to navigate this world.
Each one she places in your palm and
each one she covers with soil.
She tells you, you must carry this seed until it sprouts,
and then plant it, so that it can bloom.
Reluctantly you listen, carrying soil in your palms.
It is timeworn and your hands young and heavy.

Suns pass, Moons fall, and still in your palm, sits the seed.

When it finally sprouts you rejoice,
smiling down at it in your hands.
You place it in your garden, alongside other seedlings.
Some have grown.
Some have not.
None have bloomed.
The seeds, your mother confides in you, are a *gift*.
Not from her,
but from her mother,
and her mother before her.
This is why the soil is old, she explains –
it is the generational soil from our tree.

Years later she smiles, you will revisit this garden.
It will be filled with flowers, you beam.

With all the patience of a mother, she looks at you.
Each seed has its time-
some take years,
some take decades,
and some never bloom.
But when a seed blooms you will feel it inside of you,
deep where you have planted its seed.
What will that mean? you ask her.
It means that I have shared with you something I learned whilst
walking through this lifetime.
It means that whilst walking in your own lifetime,
you have found me,
and the guidance your family handed down to you.
You beam, and in the distance of your garden,
a flower starts to bloom.

A DAUGHTER'S INNOCENCE

The day my father left me
by the airport doors,

he kissed me on the mouth.
He squeezed my lungs and told me he loved me.

That he had never not loved me.

That he had given me my name
but that I had given him meaning.

I saw the oceans drain from his eyes
I saw the small fires in his heart,

as if I had doused him in gasoline and set him alight.

My mother took my hand and led me away,

and I curse the ignorance of a daughter's innocence.
But now I am a woman
and had you not died,

I promise you
I would have doused my own heart in gasoline
and set myself alight with you.

DEEP WITHIN OUR BELLIES

There are stories written
in my Imaa's palms.
Etched in each line,
worn thin over time.
They trace my face,
caressing me with tales,
entrusting me with history.
Assigning me with stories
that come not from the books
but from deep within our bellies.
Yes, there are stories written
in my Imaa's palms.

SISTER SISTER

The best parts of me
are my sisters
who fanned the winds
against my shoulders
for me to feel
these wings.

For you
I'd take the skies captive
and slit the throat
of a night
that thought
to blind you.

PHONECALLS FROM HARARE

My mother keeps books by her nightstand,
bible verses and prayers.
She stumbles through their pages
when she cannot sleep.
She is not by her children,
she is by herself.
In the night she awakes, and cannot rest her mind.

On the phone she tells me what she dreams of,
that one day she would like to send me money in lump
sum so that I could on a whim, buy anything I wanted,
anything I might like.
She apologizes,
she is sorry that she could not give more,
that she cannot afford for us to be together.
That all these years later and it is still hard.

I do not tell her
that there are nights I lay awake
thinking of how to repay her
for the world she placed at my feet
for the fertile soil in me she tended to
with bare and tired
that the best parts of me belong to her
and how my lungs crumple each time she speaks of
giving more.

BARE FOR ME YOUR ROOTS

And so I asked her
"tell me of the soil"
The soil from which she grew
"Let me know where you were planted,
the scent of rain and dew"

Tell me who bathed you,

who holds you whilst you stand?
If I sent you where your heart was
describe the ground on which you'd land.

Paint for me your stories
bare for me your roots
Show me where your soul blooms,
where your mind
 bears fruit.

YOU CANNOT EAT WORDS

You cannot eat words, she said.
No matter how sweet they taste.
No matter how soft they feel.

Love does not provide dear girl,
Love is not all.

Auntie you know not his love,
How it nourishes and fills.
How his kindness shelters,
embraces and lifts.

No, you know not his love,
love that need not give its last dime
because it gives you more
you know not the texture of love,
beyond survival.

MARKS

"There are marks on our daughter's face!"
"Yes, they have marked her young!"
"They have hugged her in blood!"

And loved her with glass,
        all to keep her here,
                by us.
"And now?"
"And now the Gods will not want her;"
"*A daughter who is scarred....*
"They might let us raise her,"

And she can grow here besides us
        with her skin that
            tumbles over skin.

"We told her to mark the others"
yes, but they were warmer than rain
too beautiful for here,
she could not.
She stopped us.

And so the Gods took them,
just after,

just after they arrived.

So soon,
Smiling like sun,
    Far too warm for here
       too cold for us
          without them.

LANGUAGE

When they came
they heard our songs,
but blocked their ears to the sound.
They saw us draped in our custom
and blinded their eyes to the sight.
They heard our names,
but let ego rob them of meaning,
for they had it waiting.
They came not to hear
nor to see.
They came armed in confirmation,
and with that they stole the earth
from beneath our feet,

tore our names from our tongues,
bled the stories out from our stomachs,
cut the hands of our elders

and displayed them on holy ground.
Until flies lay seed in palms
that once held us.
And so with new tongues
we spoke their names
with no meaning.

ELMINA

Elmina your name is heavy;

a sour taste along your shores.
A tightness in your spaces
scratches scarred along your walls.
There's a sin that creeps in silence,
a stifled cry that could not scream,
Emina your name hangs heavy
on this mind

oh so it seems.

ISHTUDU'S POEM

Sister, you are gentle,
you are pastel sun inside,
there is devotion to your footsteps
honey dripping through your pride
In your anger breaths rainfall
the kind that pours on heat-filled days
you're the heart that beats outside me,
in answered prayers you were made

GLOSSARY

Adinkra- The Adinkra are a set of value-based symbols in Ghana that carry significance in their meaning. Adinkra symbols today are mostly used in fabrics, architecture, jewelry, and rites of passage.

Elmina- A castle in Ghana erected by the Portuguese in 1482, and later used a trading post by colonizers in the Trans-Atlantic slave trade. It is the oldest European building South of the Sahara.

Harmattan -A dry and dusty season in West Africa that usually occurs between November and March.

Imaa - Word for Grandmother.

Ishtudu - The name given to my youngest sibling.

ACKNOWLEDGEMENTS

There are specific individuals I would like to thank for their constant love, encouragement, and support in the process of putting together this collection.

My family, who have given me such a foundation of strength in my writing. For all the lessons on unconditional love you have embedded in me and for all the times you put that into practice. To Ishtudu, Ioan, Jameel, Kukua, Baaba, Araba, Aunty Mo, and mum. I love you all endlessly.

To my chosen family. The ones who clapped for me when I doubted myself and reminded me of all the worldly possibilities within me. You have been my anchors and my wings.

Finally, to my family no longer with me in body. To Imaa and Grandad, for grounding me in where I come from. And to my late father, Peter. Thank you for instilling in me such a base of unwavering love. For the stories you told me, for the truths you told me, and for holding me and saying there is nothing I could do or be that could stop you from loving me.

ABOUT THE ARTIST

Kuukua Wilson is an illustrator and Fine Artist. She received her B.F.A in visual arts for painting and drawing from Kennesaw State University in Georgia, then continued on to her Master's in Scientific illustration at Maastricht University in The Netherlands. Currently working as a freelance illustrator, she loves creating bright and colorful visuals and images for a variety of platforms and purposes including science, education, research, and culture.

Printed in Great Britain
by Amazon

55904507R00036